LOVE LETTER TO AMERICA

TOMAS SCHUMAN

LOVE LETTER TO AMERICA

Copyright © 1984 - Tomas Schuman

Edited by Bill White

OoB Edition

Copyright © 2021 – WireNews Limited

ISBN: 9798736867394

All rights reserved. No part of this book may be reproduced in any form or by any electronic or mechanical means, including information storage and retrieval systems, without the permission in writing from the publisher, except by reviewers, who may quote brief passages in a review.

Publisher
Origin of Books
(an imprint of WireNews Limited)
www.originofbooks.com

Tel: 0730 814 5905
Fax: 0131 202 0620
Edinburgh, Scotland

EDITOR'S NOTE

Love Letter to America was originally published in 1984. This *Origin of Books* edition has been only lightly edited to correct some of the more egregious mistakes left by the former publishers. I have tried, as much as possible, to retain the original flavor and unique personality of the author.

— Bill White

CONTENTS

FOREWORD	7
MY LIFE STORY	13
PRELUDE TO SUBVERSION	28
THE FOUR STAGES OF SUBVERSION	35
STAGE ONE: DEMORALIZATION	38
THE THREE LEVELS OF DEMORALIZATION	45
IDEAS RULE THE WORLD	45
'MASS' EDUCATION	51
LORDS OF PUBLIC OPINION	54
ADDICTIVE 'MASS CULTURE'	58
THE SECOND LEVEL OF DEMORALIZATION: STRUCTURES	61
LEVEL THREE: UNHEALTHY BODY — UNHEALTHY MIND	68
STAGE TWO: DESTABILIZATION	74
POWER STRUGGLE	75
STAGE THREE: CRISIS	78
NORMALIZATION: THE FOURTH AND LAST STAGE	80
ABOUT THE AUTHOR	83

FOREWORD

Dear Americans,

My name is Tomas David Schuman. I am what you may call a "defector" from the USSR, and I have a message for you: I love you very much. I love all of you — Liberals and Conservatives, "decadent capitalists" and "oppressed masses", blacks and whites and browns and yellows, rednecks and intellectuals. For me, you are the people who created the most unique nation, the most unique country and society in the history of mankind, — by no means, a perfect one, but let's face it — the most free, affluent, and just nation in today's world.

I am not alone in this love. People all over the Earth, whether they praise America or bitterly criticize her, look upon you as the only hope for mankind's survival and the last stronghold of freedom. Some may not think in these idealistic terms, but they certainly enjoy the fruits of your civilization, often forgetting to be grateful for them. Millions of people in the so-called "socialist camp" or in the "Third World" literally owe their lives to America.

As a war-time child. I survived partly thanks to such "decadent capitalist" (as the Soviets say) things as "Spam" meat, condensed milk and egg powder that were supplied

LOVE LETTER TO AMERICA

to my country by the USA through the lend-lease program of World War II. In the Soviet Union we secretly but proudly called ourselves "the Spam generation". Too prosaic? Who cares about "Spam" in today's USA, apart from "underprivileged" welfare recipients? Well, for me these foods are not merely the nostalgic delight of my troubled childhood, but rather, a symbol of love from a friend when I was in need. No amount of communist propaganda against America has ever been able to convince me that the United States out to "colonize and exploit". I will tell you — many people have been more than willing to be "exploited" the American way. For what other reason have thousands risked their lives, gone to unimaginable troubles, left behind their families their motherland and traditional ways of life to come to America? Have you ever heard of "illegal aliens" risking their lives crossing the border at midnight into Socialist USSR? Or the "boat people" swimming oceans and drowning by the thousands just to reach the shores of Communist China? Or defectors like me, leaving behind relative affluence and risking bullets in the back to join the "progressive workers' paradise" in Russia? No, we all come here to America, obviously willing to be "exploited by capitalists" and enjoy "oppression" together with you. Because we believe and KNOW — America IS A BETTER place.

I am writing this not to please you with words you want to hear. The rest of my message may be more unpleasant to you than even Communist propaganda, or more offensive than the speeches of "leaders" in Kremlin. But as a true friend of America, I want to help.

My dear friends, I think you are in big trouble. Whether you believe it or not, YOU ARE AT WAR. And you may lose this war very soon, together with all your affluence and freedoms, unless you start defending yourselves. I hope you have noticed on your color televisions that there is in fact war going on right now all over this planet. This war has many faces, but it's all the same — it is war. Some call it "national liberation", some title it "class struggle" or "political terrorism". Others call it "anticolonialism" or "struggle for majority rule". Some even come up with such fancy names as "war of patriotic forces" or "peace movement". I call it World Communist Aggression. I know what I am talking about, because I was on the side of the aggressor before I decided to take YOUR side. I do not believe — I KNOW — that in this war no one is being "liberated, decolonized or made equal", as Soviet doctrine proclaims. You may notice, if you give yourselves the trouble to observe, that the only "equality" and "liberation" this war produces are the equality of death and the "liberation" from freedom. Look at Russia, Poland, Hungary, Afghanistan — would you say the people of those countries celebrated and rejoiced when the Soviets brought them equality and liberation? Of course not. We must take a clear and honest look at what Soviet "liberation"

LOVE LETTER TO AMERICA

means.

This war of Communist World Aggression is not fought against some mythological "capitalists" as Communist propaganda claims. No, my dear friends, this war is fought against YOU — personally. Communist wars of world aggression are not fought for liberty and equality. We have thousands of unequivocal examples of the horrendous human suffering, torture and mass death that occur after a Soviet "liberation". The final stage of Communist aggression — military confrontation — has extraordinarily little to do with rivalry for territorial or geopolitical gains to free and liberate. Communist world aggression is a total war against humanity and human civilization. In Communist propaganda terms, this is "the final struggle for the victory of Communism".

The driving force of this war has little to do with natural aspirations of people for better lives and greater freedoms. If at all, these aspirations are being used and taken advantage of by the manipulators and progenitors of the war. The real driving force of this war of aggression is IDEOLOGY — something you cannot eat, wear or store for a "rainy day". An integral part of this war of ideology is IDEOLOGICAL SUBVERSION — the process of changing the perception of reality in the minds of millions of peoples all over the world. The late comrade Andropov, the former head of the Soviet KGB called this war of Communist aggression, "the final struggle for the MINDS and hearts of the people".

The reason that I am so certain of the real goal of Communist aggression is that I was a part and an unwilling instrument of Soviet subversion tactics. Having been trained and used by the KGB for their global ideological subversion campaign, I have some first-hand knowledge about the people behind this war and the methods they use. I know very well the way the Communists, whom the Western media call "freedom fighters" and "rebels", operate. I know their mentality and their methods, I know their ultimate goals, which are far from the liberty, equality, and freedom they verbally espouse. Because I have seen the tragic consequences of this war of ideological subversion, I would like to offer some suggestions as to how we in the United States can DEFEND ourselves against this deadly war and how we can SURVIVE in this "final struggle for minds and hearts".

"What's in it for Tomas Schuman," you may ask. Well, I have asked myself. What do I get for defecting from the winning side (the Soviets) ... and joining the losers? (I hope I do not have to tell you, that at least a dozen countries have succumbed to the Communists since my defection.) Dear friends, I have gained nothing materially from my defection. What I have gained is a firm commitment to the United

LOVE LETTER TO AMERICA

States as the last real frontier of freedom. This is it, dear Americans, your country (and mine now) will be the last to be "liberated" by Marxists, socialists, and domestic "do-gooders". If the "liberationists" succeed in bringing their "New Order" to America, chances are you and I will meet in front of a firing squad — or worse in a "re-education" forced labor camp in the Alaskan Peoples Democratic Republic.

You have too many concrete examples of what Communist "liberation" has done for other countries to believe that I am wrong when I warn you that we are on the brink of disaster. From one that has lived, worked, and seen first-hand the realities of day-to-day life in a communist/ socialist state — you must wake up now and start defending the rights and freedoms you now have. No matter how many problems you think the U.S. may have, believe me when I say that they are nothing in comparison to the troubles you will experience if the U.S. continues to agree and sympathize with communist/socialist doctrines.

I have made my choice to be with YOU, the nation I love. I have risked my life like many others, to tell you of my life and experiences within a Communist state. You have nothing to risk by listening to me and making up your mind as to whether I am a "cold war paranoic", as your media calls me, or whether my message makes sense.

The choice is yours.

MY LIFE STORY

I was born Yuri Alexandrovich Bezmenov in Moscow in 1939.

My father was an officer of the Soviet Army General Staff. As inspector of the Land Forces, he was stationed in "fraternal countries" such as Mongolia, Cuba, and East Germany. If he were alive today, he would most likely be checking the status of Soviet troops in Angola, Ethiopia, Yemen, Syria, Vietnam, Cambodia, Nicaragua, and the ever-growing number of other "liberated" countries.

I was brought up under the shadow of comrade Stalin, to the echo of the World War II. As a loyal and patriotically minded young Communist, I loved my country, good or bad. However, unlike certain Western intellectuals and liberals, I did not require half a century to realize that the "leaders" of my country are self-imposed dictators — mass murderers, and that the ideology of Marxism-Leninism is a false system that produces none of the advantages or benefits of the "worker's paradise" that it promises. It was a simple matter for me to compare the Soviet propaganda claims given to all

Tomas Schuman dreaming about exotic Asia as a schoolboy

LOVE LETTER TO AMERICA

Russian citizens of glorious "socialist achievements" with the surrounding realities — early morning bread lines, because we had so little to eat; the frequents arrests of "enemies of the people" and the omnipresent fear of the KGB.

Because of my war-time childhood spent in the Asian section of the USSR, I developed an early affection for the oriental way of life and at the age of 17 after graduating from elementary school, I entered the Institute of Oriental Languages, an affiliate of Moscow State University. The Institute was under the direct control of KGB and Communist Central Committee — an elitist nest for future Soviet diplomats, foreign correspondents, and spies.

At the Institute, while studying several foreign language and mass media, I was required to also take compulsory military training. During training, we students were taught how to play "strategic war games" using the maps of foreign countries. Civil Defense and anti-nuclear training were also essential parts of our education. In addition, we took

Tomas Schuman as a student at the Oriental Languages Institute

"interrogation classes" which were designed to teach us how to interrogate prisoners of war. We were instructed to interrogate prisoners as to their reaction to a Soviet nuclear strike aimed at their country — it was for me a bizarre experience. Upon graduating, I was sent to India as a translator for the Soviet Economic Aid Group which was building oil refineries in two Indian states. Here, during my first foreign assignment, I realized the great discrepancy between my country's proclaimed goals of "selfless fraternal cooperation" and the actual ruthless exploitation of India by Soviet neo-colonialists. As an example of this exploitation, the Soviets, in purchasing Indian manufactured goods, would pay the Indians only in rubles.

I was dreaming about exotic Asia as a schoolboy (below); and as a student at Oriental Languages Institute (above).

Unfortunately, rubles are non-convertible currency on the international market, meaning that the Indian manufacturer would be unable to purchase anything on the international market with his Soviet rubles. On the other hand, the Soviets would take the Indian manufactured goods and sell them at a substantial profit on the international market for "hard currency" such as dollars or pounds which are easily negotiable. So basically, the Indian manufacturer received only a fraction of the actual worth of his product, while the Soviets reaped the rewards of their duplicity.

Is it that the Indians are stupid, ignorant people, that they allow the Soviets to deceive them in this manner? On the

LOVE LETTER TO AMERICA

contrary — for the most part, they are innocent victims of one of the world's most sophisticated con games — Ideological Subversion. They have been psychologically manipulated through media, politics, etc., into believing that the Soviets are their friends who are protecting them from the "Western imperialists." This same subversion game is being played all over the world — even in America, KGB influence in our media, politics and nearly every phase of our life has produced a growing conviction on the part of many Americans that we are the "bad guys" — again I must remind you that to date, there has never been a single defection from the United States. The Soviets have produced a ludicrous global lie that people are believing — why? Because the tactics of ideological subversion work.

Even after witnessing the ruthless tactics used by my country, I still naively hoped that things would turn out for the better eventually.

After all, I was a product of the post-Stalin era of "thaw" and liberalization started by Khrushchev. I believed in "Socialism with a human face". That faith was shattered irreparably only five years later, when I witnessed the brutal Soviet military intervention into "fraternal" Czechoslovakia in 1968.

After completing my first assignment in India, in 1965 I was recalled to Moscow and immediately joined the "Novosti Press Agency (Novosti means "news" in Russian language) —

the biggest and most powerful propaganda, espionage and ideological front of the KGB. I was employed by Novosti as an apprentice for their classified department of 'Political Publications' (GRPP) under comrade Norman Borodin. After working a short time, I discovered that about 75% of the Novosti's staffers were KGB officers; the other 25% were "co-optees", or KGB freelance writers / public relations officers; informers like myself. The other interesting fact I discovered was that there was no "news" at Novosti. My main job, apart from writing, editing, and translating propaganda materials to be planted in foreign media, was accompanying delegations of Novosti's guests — journalists, editors, publishers, writers, politicians, and businessmen from foreign countries on tours of the USSR or to international conferences held in the Soviet Union. As a freelance journalist, I did absolutely no writing or news coverage at all. After several months I was formally recruited by the KGB as an informer, while still maintaining my position as a Novosti journalist. My work with the KGB entailed combining my journalistic duties with the collection of intelligence data, and the spreading of "disinformation" to foreign countries for the purposes of Soviet propaganda and subversion. It was only a matter of time before the KGB realized that my personal friendships with guests of Novosti Press Agency could also be utilized for their operations.

Why did I allow myself to be recruited? There really is no

simple answer. For one thing, a Soviet journalist cannot simply say "no" to the KGB. If he wants to remain alive, free, pursue his career and travel abroad, he simply must cooperate with the KGB, or suffer the consequences.

Tomas Schuman (left) with a microphone recording a propaganda "social event" with the USSR Embassy officials and Mrs Indira Gandhi - willing participant of Soviet propaganda operations in India

Secondly, apart from monetary and material gains, a Soviet journalist co-opted (hired) by the KGB has a rare chance to become IMPORTANT in his own country, and in 1965, the USSR was still my country. Many of my colleagues, both cynicists and true patriots, joined the KGB, naively believing that they could promote themselves to the higher positions of power, while maintaining their secretly kept moral principles and disguising their actual disgust of the system. By the time most of them realized that 'power corrupts' and that allegiance with the Soviet Communist power corrupts absolutely — it was too late. Most of my former colleagues are now firmly entrenched in the 'privileged class I and their humanistic ideals have all been traded one by one for small comforts such as a private car (a rare thing in the USSR), a free apartment, a country house ("dacha"), free trips abroad and freedom to socialize with foreigners, none of which would be possible or available to the average Russian worker.

So, despite my early dislike of the Soviet Communist system, I joined the KGB, hoping in some way to 'outsmart them', to play the game until I could see more clearly how to proceed. My rapid promotion followed. I was once again assigned to India, this time as a USSR press-officer and a 'P. R.' agent for the KGB. Because of my knowledge of India and her languages — Hindi and Urdu, I became deeply involved in the KGB operations in India. I was directed by my superiors to establish the Soviet 'sphere of influence' slowly but surely in India.

In addition to the bribery and corruption of Indian officials, blackmail, and intrusion into the internal affairs of India, the Soviets went one step further in their 'brotherly assistance' to India. In 1969 by a secret directive of the Central Committee of the CPSU (Communist Party of the Soviet Union), all

LOVE LETTER TO AMERICA

embassies of the USSR all over the world, including India, opened a new secret department innocently titled "Research and Counter-Propaganda Group". I became a deputy chief of that department, working under a KGB officer, comrade. Valeri Neyev.

It did not take me long to discover that our group was engaged in, neither "research" nor "counter-propaganda": behind locked doors we accumulated intelligence from various sources, including Indian informers and agents, regarding virtually EVERY important and politically significant citizen of India — members of Parliament, civil servicemen, military and public figures, media people, businessmen, university professors, radical or otherwise students and writers — in other words EVERYONE instrumental in shaping the PUBLIC OPINION and policies of the nation. Those who were "friendly "and ready to invite the Soviet expansionist policy into their own country were promoted to higher positions of power, affluence, and prestige through various operations by KG B-Novosti. Large groups, of the so-called "progressive and sober-thinking" Indians were on a regular basis, generously supplied with duty-free booze from the embassy stocks. Soviet sympathizers were invited to the USSR for free trips and numerous "international conferences" where they not only received substantial sums of money in the form of "literary awards" or "Nehru Peace and Friendship" prizes but were also medically treated for VD or hernias acquired in the perpetual "class struggle" against "American imperialism". Those who refused to be "flexible" and take a voluntary role in this cruel farce were thoroughly character-assassinated in the sensation-hungry media and press.

Let me give you an example of how the KGB uses the information it collects. One day in 1968, I was routinely scanning through the backlog of USA Information Service releases and classified documentation, generously supplied to us by our Indian and American "friends". In one of the dispatches, I read that the South Vietnamese city of Hue had been captured by the Hanoi Communists. When it was re-captured by the US Army and allied forces, only two days later, the CIA discovered to their horror that several thousand Vietnamese — teachers, priests, Buddhists, businessmen, and educated citizens — everyone who was "pro-American", had been rounded up by the invaders and IN ONE NIGHT, taken out of the city limits and executed collectively. Some were shot. Others, with their hands tied by electric wire, were found with their skulls crushed-in by shovels and iron bars. "How could they possibly have located all of these people within only a few hours in a large city?" — the Americans wondered. I thought I knew the answer.

Long before the invasion there was an extensive network of Communist informers working under the guidance of the

LOVE LETTER TO AMERICA

Soviet embassy in Hanoi — that is under the KGB. The Communists filed every bit of information: addresses, personal habits, political affiliations, expressed ideas, unexpressed thoughts revealed in informal and private conversations, even the names and addresses of relatives, friends, even lovers and mistresses of the future victims of "liberation". After reading the news release I was sick, physically, with the realization that the department I was working for in New Delhi was engaged in the same activity that had been used in the city of Hue. I realized fully that I was a part of a heinous crime against our host country. Adding to my nausea, I discovered that some of our files contained data of a personal nature; intimate information such as "sexual preferences" e.g., homosexualism, of certain Indian VIPs — even radicals and Communists openly sympathetic to Soviet policies. Were they also listed for execution if a Soviet-backed revolution in India should occur?

My frustration was compounded by my KGB supervisor who coached me in a fatherly tone: "Don't bother with these prostitutes, the Indian Communists Don't waste your time with them. There is nothing more dangerous than disillusioned "true believers" in Communism. They turn into the most bitter enemies and counter-revolutionaries — aim higher - at respectable "conservative" well-established "capitalists" and pro-American elements!" So, as you can see, the KGB/ Soviets have absolutely no respect for the majority of their new "converts".

One event that solidified my increasing horror of KGB tactics concerned one of my closest Indian friends, a journalist who represented one of the most influential newspapers in India.

When I discovered that my friend had been targeted for a KGB character assassination campaign, I felt a tremendous desire to escape from the USSR embassy immediately and to confide to my Indian friend the situation confronting him, and my desire to break my ties with the KGB — which meant defection. However, such an impulse scheme could have hardly succeeded. The Indian government, under strong pressure from the Soviet embassy, had adopted a law which stated that no defector from any country has a right of political asylum in ANY embassy in the territory of the Republic of India. This masterpiece of political hypocrisy had been created by Mrs. Indira Gandhi after Stalin's daughter Svetlana, defected to the West while residing in India. Because of this situation I knew full well that my defection would not be a simple matter, and as a result, it required a carefully thought-out plan. To be caught by the KGB while attempting defection would mean that I would be forcefully returned to Russian and imprisoned — perhaps worse. I therefore resolved to wait until I had formed a definite plan for my escape.

LOVE LETTER TO AMERICA

However, my patience was running thin. One of the last straws for me was a story I heard from one of my KGB colleagues: I learned that the Soviet Union was importing Soviet trained subversives to East Pakistan in preparation for a revolution there. My colleague further informed me that Soviet cases marked "printed matter — to Dacca University" stored in the basement of the USSR consulate in Calcutta were accidentally discovered to contain, not university texts, but rather Kalashnikov guns (AK-47s) and ammunition for the anticipated communist revolution in Pakistan.

The KGB and Indian Police were looking for a wrong person

TOMAS SCHUMAN

This is how Tomas Schuman looked at the time of defection

This incident occurred in December of 1969. Two months later I "disappeared" from the USSR embassy in New Delhi. To avoid detection by the Indian Police and the KGB, I had disguised myself as an American "hippie". This method of defection was a guaranteed success — no -KGB detective in his "right mind" would have thought to look for a missing Soviet diplomat among the crowds of long-haired, bearded, barefoot, hashish-smoking Americans who had invaded India in search of 'enlightenment'. And so, I escaped to the West. I landed successfully in Canada in July 1970.

There, I studied history and political science, taught Russian language and literature, and worked for the Canadian Broadcasting Corporation as an announcer/ producer for

LOVE LETTER TO AMERICA

Radio-Canada International (an equivalent of the 'Voice of America'). I was later forced to resign from my position with the Canadian Broadcasting Corporation due to a complaint made by the USSR ambassador to Canada to the Canadian government stating that I was anti-Soviet.

Realizing that I did not have the support of the Canadian government for having made my choice not to perform acts for the KGB and Soviet Russia that violated my sense of justice and right action; I came to America.

Presently I am a freelance writer and political analyst, trying — though not always successfully, to awaken the Western populace to the realities of life under the Soviet system and to the IDEOLOGICAL SUBVERSION that is being practiced upon them daily.

It is my hope that this booklet, and the follow-up booklets that I am now writing will make clear to all who read them, the real facts behind the barrage of false media, ideas and information from the Soviet Union that represent the Communist state as a "workers' paradise".

Believe me when I say, having lived through it — it was no paradise.

TOMAS SCHUMAN

Two different attitudes to India: Tomas Schuman socializing with an Indian student and thinking about marrying an Indian girl following the Marxist slogan: 'Proletarian of all the world, unite'. The Communist Party had a different plan for Schuman. He had to marry a Soviet interpreter.

Soviet Diplomat Y. Ashitkov always rolled up the windows of his car to avoid the 'smell of those stinking Indians'.

PRELUDE TO SUBVERSION

All warfare is based primarily on deception of an enemy. Fighting on a battlefield is the most primitive way of making war. There is no art higher than to destroy your enemy without a fight - by SUBVERTING anything of value in enemy's country. — Sun-Tzu, (Chinese philosopher 500 B.C.)

The art of duping the masses into doing things to their own disadvantage and making them believe it is "the will of people" is as ancient as mankind itself.

The essence of subversion is best expressed in the famous Marxist slogan, (if you substitute "proletarians" for a more appropriate word): "Useful idiots of the world — UNITE!

To achieve the desired effect, the subverter must first — make idiots out of normal people, and DIVIDE them, before turning the people into a homogenized mass of useful and united idiots. Tanks and missiles may or may not be needed at final stage.

For the time being they are simply the means of terrorizing people into inaction and submission.

500 years before Christ, the Chinese military strategist Sun Tzu

formulated the principle of subversion this way:

1. Cover with ridicule all the valid traditions in your opponent's country;

2. Implicate their leaders in criminal affairs and turn them over to the scorn of their populace at the right time;

3. Disrupt the work of their government by every means;

4. Do not shun the aid of the lowest and most despicable individuals of your enemy's country;

5. Spread disunity and dispute among the citizens;

6. Turn the young against the old;

7. Be generous with promises and rewards to collaborators and accomplices;

Sound familiar? About 2500 years later we can read this very same instruction in a secret document, allegedly authored by the Communist International for their "young revolutionaries". The document is titled "Rules of Revolution":

1. Corrupt the young, get them interested in sex, take them away from religion. Make them superficial and enfeebled;

2. Divide the people into hostile groups by constantly harping on controversial issues of no importance;

LOVE LETTER TO AMERICA

3. Destroy people's faith in their national leaders by holding the latter up for contempt, ridicule, and disgrace;

4. Always preach democracy but seize power as fast and as ruthlessly as possible;

5. By encouraging government extravagances, destroy its credit, produce years of inflation with rising prices and general discontent;

6. Incite unnecessary strikes in vital industries, encourage civil disorders and foster a lenient and soft attitude on the part of the government towards such disorders;

7. Cause breakdown of the old moral virtues: honesty, sobriety, self-restraint, faith in the pledged word;

I cannot vouch for authenticity of this document, which, according to American conservative media was captured by the Allied forces after WW II in defeated Germany, in Dusseldorf. But I can assure you, that these "rules" are almost a literal interpretation of those "theories and practices" which I learned from my KGB superiors and colleagues within the 'Novosti' Press Agency.

Yes, I am aware of the possibility, that nothing I write here is a "sensational revelation" to many of you. What I did was simply to structure my knowledge and experience with the Soviet subversion system into a simple and graphic record.

To help you to get an overall picture of the SUBVERSION process, let me first outline for you the movement of a target nation from the state of "open society" to a "closed" one. This outline is taken from secret, not so secret and non-secret Marxist literature: An "open society" is the one you are living now. You can work in it, or choose not to work, have private property, or have nothing at all, love it or leave it, criticize it without fear of being declared an "enemy of people." It is a society, based on free individual initiative and the free market system.

All you must do to "screw up" the status quo of a free nation, is to borrow ON E false idea from the ideology of a communist or totalitarian government. For the sake of simplicity, I have chosen the idea of "egalitarianism". "People born equal therefore must be equal".

Sounds great. But look at yourselves. Were you born equal? Some of you weighed 7 pounds at birth, others 6 or 5 . . . Are you NOW equal?

In any way? Physically, mentally, emotionally, racially, spiritually?

Some are tall and dumb, others — short, bald, and clever. Now, let's figure out what will happen if we LEGISLATE EQUALITY, and make the concept of "equality" a cornerstone and pillar of socioeconomical and political system. All right? You don't have to be a great economist or sociologist to foresee that some of the people who are "less equal" would demand as much as those who are "more equal" BY LAW!

Aha, now you've got it. There will be some who get more for GIVING less and take advantage of those, who are even "less equal", say, in the art of TAKING. And to avoid the squabble for "equal redistribution" you will have to introduce a THIRD FORCE — the State. Why? Because people were never equal, are not equal and if God wanted us to be equal, He would probably have made us equal.

No. He provided a difference. "Vive la Difference!" — said the French before the French Revolution. And they were right.

The beauty of the best, most successful political/ economic system, created by the Fathers of America has nothing to do with LEGISLATED or enforced equality. The American Republic is based on the principle of EQUAL OPPORTUNITIES for UNEQUAL and very much DIFFERENT and diverse individuals to develop their abilities and to coexist in mutually beneficial cooperation. And that is entirely different story. That much I knew even from the Soviet textbooks of American history.

Now let's move faster. People who have declared

themselves to be equal will inevitably come to expect more for their individual needs, which sooner or later will tragically come to conflict with the "un-equal" reality. That will automatically produce discontent. Unhappy and discontent masses are less productive than those who are happy being what they are and making the best of it. Decreased productivity, as we all know, leads to such unpleasant things as inflation, un-employment, and recession. These, in turn, cause social unrest and instability, both economic and political.

Chronic instability breeds radicalism as a means of solving problems. Radicalism is the precondition of a power struggle which may (and has often) resulted in violent and forceful replacements of power structures. If the situation deteriorates badly, this replacement takes ugly forms of internal civil war, or revolution, or invitation of a "friendly and fraternal" neighbor, and finally ends up in the traditional way — namely, state control. Depending on maturity of a nation, and the amount (or absence) of common sense, this control will manifest itself in the creation of a "closed society" — the opposite of what we had in the beginning. Borders are closed, censorship of the media is established, "irritants" and "enemies" of the state are executed, etc.

This is my 'simplistic' and highly 'unscientific' outline of the events which have happened in many countries of the

LOVE LETTER TO AMERICA

world. Any nation can do this to herself without any help from comrades Andropov and Brezhnev and their numerous KGB agents. Any one of you can easily observe this vicious chain of events by simply reading your newspapers regularly or even watching the TV.

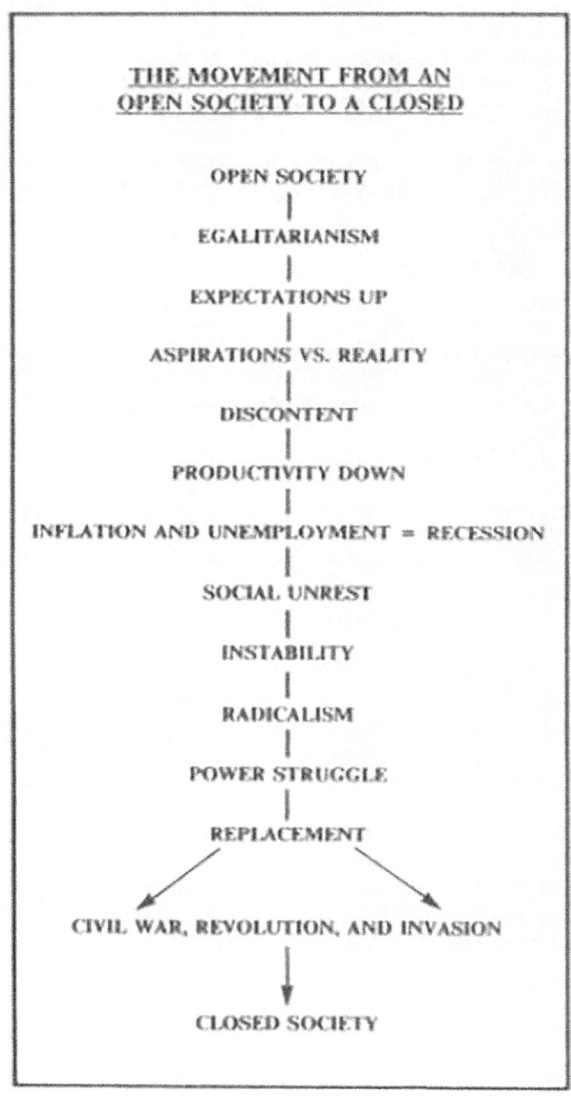

THE FOUR STAGES OF SUBVERSION

What many of you do not see, is the second "chain" of events which I graphically represent in the chart (previous page) of the FOUR STAGES OF SUBVERSION:

1. DEMORALIZATION

2. DESTABILIZATION

3. CRISIS

4. NORMALIZATION

What has all this to do with the KGB? Very simple: these are the 'most favorable conditions' listed in any Marxist textbook of revolutionary struggle. I have simply placed them in chronological order and divided them into three vertical columns: the areas of application, the methods of subversion and the expected (or achieved) results.

In the context of the USA, most of these nasty things are done to America by Americans . . . with the IDEOLOGICAL help of the Communist subverters. Most of the actions are overt, legitimate, and easily identifiable. The only trouble is — they are "stretched in time".

In other words, the process of subversion is such a long-term process that an average individual, due to the short time

LOVE LETTER TO AMERICA

span of his historical memory, is unable to perceive the process of subversion as a CONSISTENT and willful effort. That is exactly how it is intended to be: like the small hand of your watch. You know it moves, but you CAN NOT SEE it moving.

The main principle of ideological subversion is TURNING A STRONGER FORCE AGAINST ITSELF. Just like in the Japanese martial arts: you do not stop the blow of a heavier more powerful enemy with an equally forceful blow. You may simply hurt your hand. Instead, you catch the striking fist with your hand and PULL the enemy in the direction of his blow until he crashes into a wall or any other heavy object in his way.

America is obviously a "stronger force" that Communism is unable to defeat. But it is possible to conquer this nation using the preconditions I have described, created by Americans themselves, and diverting America's attention away from these mortally dangerous preconditions. The situation is like a house, the owners of which have stored explosives and inflammable materials INSIDE. To destroy this house the enemy does not have to intrude physically into it. It is enough to start a fire next door and wait till the wind blows in the right direction. Meanwhile the enemy may "throw in some great ideas" for the owners to argue about to take their attention off the actual fire: environmental protection, gay liberation or emancipation of house pets are the types of non-critical arguments that divert America's attention from the real danger.

Smart people would notice the fire and remove the inflammable objects and materials BEFORE the house catches the fire.

THE SUBVERSION PROCESS

AREAS	METHODS	RESULTS
DEMORALIZATION (15 TO 20 YEARS)		
IDEAS		
1. RELIGION	POLITICIZE, COMMERCIALIZE, ENTERTAINMENT	DEATH WISH
2. EDUCATION	PERMISSIVENESS, RELATIVITY	IGNORANCE
3. MEDIA	MONOPOLIZE, MANIPULATE, DISCREDIT, NON-ISSUES	UNINFORMED MYOPIA
4. CULTURE	FALSE HEROES AND ROLE MODELS	ADDICTIVE FADS, MASS
STRUCTURE		
1. LAW AND ORDER	LEGISLATIVE, NOT MORAL	MISTRUST 'JUSTICE'
2. SOCIAL RELATIONS	RIGHTS VS. OBLIGATIONS	LESS INDIVIDUAL RESPONS.
3. SECURITY	INTELLIGENCE, POLICE, MILITARY	DEFENSELESSNESS
4. INTERNAL POLITICS	PARTY, ANTAGONISMS	DISUNITY
5. FOREIGN	SALT — FRIENDS	ISOLATION
LIFE		
1. FAMILY, SOCIETY	BREAK UP	NO LOYALTY (STATE)
2. HEALTH	SPORTS, MEDICARE, JUNK FOOD	ENFEEBLED MASSES
3. RACE	LOWER THE UPPERS, BIBLE? GENETICS VS. ENVIRONMENT	HATRED, DIVISION
4. POPULATION	DE-LAND, URBANIZE	ALIENATION
5. LABOR	UNIONS VS. SOCIETY	VICTIMIZATION
↓		
DESTABILIZATION (2 TO 5 YEARS)		
1. POWER STRUGGLE	POPULISM, IRRESPONSIBLE POWER STRUGGLE	BIG BROTHER
2. ECONOMY	DESTRUCTION OF BARGAINING PROCESS	YIELD TO BIG BROTHER
3. SOCIETY FIRED, LAW	GRASS ROOTS PARTICIPATION	MOBOCRACY
4. FOREIGN	ISOLATION, MULTI-NATIONS, AND CENTRAL COMM.	PRESTIGE, BELLIGERENT ENCIRCLEMENT
↓		
CRISIS (2 TO 6 MONTHS)		
↓		
NORMALIZATION		

BY TOMAS SCHUMAN

This chart shows the four stages of Soviet ideological subversion: demoralization, destabilization, crisis, and normalization. The methods used by the subverter in the different areas of life produce their desired results in a country that does not resist the subversion process.

LOVE LETTER TO AMERICA

Useful idiots will keep arguing about whether it is constitutional or not to pay firefighters, or the equality of husband and wife in domestic chores (who should remove the combustibles), until the actual explosion blows their enfeebled brains all over the neighborhood.

Now, let us get back to my chart. I know it is going to be somewhat boring. But my purpose is not to entertain you but to explain what my former KGB bosses consider important for your "liberation".

STAGE ONE: DEMORALIZATION

This process has many names: psychological warfare, ideological aggression, propaganda warfare etc. The KGB calls it "Active Measures". Since my defection from the USSR embassy in 1970, I have been trying desperately to explain to the Western media, politicians, "intelligence community" and your "academic-Soviet-*ologists*" that Active Measures are more important and dangerous than classic espionage — James Bond style.

At long last, in 1983, in his new book "KGB Today" John Barron accurately and excellently described the process of demoralization, basing some of his analysis on the data supplied by another KGB defector, KGB official, Stanislav

Levchenko — incidentally, my former schoolmate from the Oriental Studies Institute who was later stationed in Tokyo, Japan under the guise of correspondent with "New Time" magazine.

Stanislav Levchenko succeeded where I failed: he brought the Active Measures to the attention of American public. The purpose of this process is to change your perception of reality to such an extent,

that even despite an abundance of information and evidence about the danger of Communism, you are unable to come to sensible conclusions in your own interests and in the interests of your nation.

John Barron ominously titled one chapter of his book, dedicated to analysis of the Active Measures, "Reality Upside Down". Excellent title! This is exactly what my KGB gurus of subversion in 'Novosti' Press Agency taught me. One of the main tactics in this process is to develop, establish and consistently enforce a set of 'double standards': one in relation to the USSR, another to the USA.

Western analysts have already pointed out the diverse tactics of "Active Measures." Some of these were exactly the ones I was trained to use while working with foreign delegations in Moscow and the USSR embassy in New Delhi: overt and covert propaganda; use of "Agents of Influence,"

LOVE LETTER TO AMERICA

faked 'International Forums' created by KGB/ Novosti to bring the atmosphere of legitimacy and respectability to Soviet operations; provoking and manipulating mass demonstrations and assemblies; spreading rumors and 'reliable information from circles close to Politburo'; forgeries of USA

Information Service press-releases; planting phony stories in local media; creating hundreds of tabloid newspapers subsidized by the USSR embassy through front organizations and fake 'advertising' companies for the purpose of 'legally' financing groups of subversives and radicals, etc. Other tactics, such as sabotage, character assassination of 'stubborn' Indians resisting Soviet subversion, terrorism, and even occasional killings of 'reactionaries and counter-revolutionaries' for the psychological effect of 'paralyzing with fear' — these also were used by my KGB colleagues from other departments of the USSR embassy.

I am less familiar with these aspects of the subversion process. My role as a 'legitimate' and overt public relations man and a 'charismatic' socializer was directed by the KGB mainly at the initial stage of subversion. After a certain period of befriending and 'cultivating' foreigners, I had to provide my KGB supervisor with my 'psychological assessment' of the target individual (or group) and pass them over to the "professionals" for further 'processing' and recruitment.

Nevertheless, I was able to reconstruct the overall picture of the process rather accurately, and, unlike the Western *Soviet-ologists*, come to more systematic and logical description of subversion.

What I offer you now is a chart as simple as a multiplication table and as complex as calculus. This is THE FIRST TIME this chart has ever been published, in its entirety.

Let us start with the first stage of DEMORALIZATION. It takes about 15 to 20 years to demoralize a nation. Why that many (or few)?

Simple: this is the minimum number of years needed to 'educate' ONE GENERATION of students in a target country (America, for example) and expose them to the ideology of the subverter. It is imperative that any sufficient challenge and counterbalance by the basic moral values and ideology of this country be limited. In absence of ANY cohesive and consistent national ideology, the task of the subverter becomes even easier. In the USA, as we all know, there is MULTIPLICITY of ideas and ideologies today, without proper emphasis on the main and basic American ideology of the original republic and the free market system. It is not even considered 'intellectual' or fashionable these days to subscribe entirely to this 'outmoded' set of ideas.

LOVE LETTER TO AMERICA

To be successful, the process of subversion at the stage of DEMORALIZATION must be always and only a TWO-WAY street which means that the target nation MUST be made a RECIPIENT — passive or active — of the IDEAS of the subverter.

Democracy is, by definition, a RECIPIENT of a multiplicity of ideologies and values, whether good or bad. Unfortunately, 'bad' ideas are often proven and revealed only after a long period of time, during which many have absorbed them and allowed them to change their nation's attitudes and behavior. Ancient Japanese rulers understood this principle very well when they virtually ISOLATED their nation from ANY foreign influence — good, bad, or neutral.

Imperial Japan was 'preserved' in its own set of historical values long enough to bring up a mature and morally stable nation able to make the change to an entirely new technological civilization with negligible damage to national fiber. More than that: the Japanese, although reluctantly, opened to Western values and surpassed the West in the shortest possible historical span since the World War II, becoming one of the greatest industrialized and technologically advanced powers in the world. Without such 'maturity' a nation may ill-conceive even the most favorable foreign influence which is clearly demonstrated by; several 'decolonized' Third World countries prematurely embracing parliamentary democracy.

But when an outside influence is purposely ill-intended, an immature nation — or a nation with a neglected indigenous ideology (America) — automatically becomes a recipient of SUBVERSION in its early stage of DEMORALIZATION.

The successful demoralization is an IRREVOCABLE process, at least for another generation. Why? Let us take an example: the semi-literate and unstable American generation of the 'crazy' 1960's is now approaching the age of 40. These people, who were too preoccupied with protesting the Vietnam war, the drug/ rock music scene, taking part in 'love-ins' etc., to study and prepare for assuming their civil responsibilities, are now in positions of power and decision-making in government, business, media, social life, entertainment (Hollywood), military, and intelligence services. Not all of them? OK, some of them are. You are STUCK with them, until they retire or resign.

You cannot fire them — it's against union regulations. You cannot, unlike the USSR, send them to Alaska, after declaring them 'enemies of people'. You cannot even openly and effectively criticize them — they have invaded the media and control public opinion. Unless you want to be called 'McCarthyistic', you cannot change their attitudes and mores. At this age, people are usually 'set' in their ways as individuals. YOU ARE STUCK with them. THEY change your

LOVE LETTER TO AMERICA

attitudes and opinions, they navigate the domestic and foreign affairs, they are making decisions and choices for YOU, whether you like it or not.

To change the direction of America's future and to return to the basic American values, proven to be efficient and productive for almost 200 years of historically unprecedented freedom and affluence, you must educate a NEW generation of Americans, this time in the spirit of patriotism and CAPITALISM. All right, you don't want to 'return'. You'd rather have something new and progressive AND constructive, to make America once again respected and loved all over the world, so that the recipients of the U.S. aid no longer shout, 'Yankee Go Home"? In any case, even if you start the education of a NEW generation of Americans RIGHT THIS MINUTE, it will take you the next 15 to 20 years to raise this new generation to the levels of power and authority. You may reduce this length of time if you can make an enormous ALL-NATION effort in an atmosphere of prevailing UNITY and CONSENSUS. It will take a miracle (or another national disaster, such as a new world war, God forbid) to make Americans embrace ONE American ideology and to act in ONE direction after decades of disunity, dispute, partisan antagonisms, and self-castigation.

Therefore, let's be realistic: the DEMORALIZATION, whether self-inflicted or imported, is usually an IRREVERSIBLE — for one generation at least — process.

THE THREE LEVELS OF DEMORALIZATION

Now, let us see the same stage of demoralization from the standpoint of the SUBVERTER. Communist manipulators divide the areas of APPLICATION of their efforts into THREE LEVELS. The process of demoralization operates simultaneously on all three levels, which I call for the sake of simplicity:

1. IDEAS (consciousness);

2. STRUCTURES (socio-political set up of a nation); and

3. LIFE (which includes all the areas of MATERIAL existence of a nation, the 'fiber of life' so to say);

IDEAS RULE THE WORLD

The level of IDEAS, the highest level of subversion, affects such vital areas as religion, education, media, and culture, to name just a few of the most important ones. If we look back in history of mankind, we may notice that the greatest upheavals and changes were caused by IDEAS, by faiths and beliefs, not by KNOWLEDGE or THINGS. Few people sacrifice their comforts and lives for such trivial things as a new car. Scientific knowledge seldom generates strong collective emotions.

LOVE LETTER TO AMERICA

Many scientists have preferred life and affluence to death for scientific truth. I have never heard of a man who would staunchly face a firing squad for the sake of defending the truth of the Law of Gravity or 2x2=4. But FAITH in the seemingly irrelevant (at the time) and immaterial teachings of Jesus Christ generated such tremendous MORAL FORCE in MILLIONS of human beings for the past TWO THOUSAND YEARS, that people willingly and happily accept violent death and tortures rather than deny their belief in Christ!

Communism and its Marxist- Leninist dogma, according to some thinkers (Dr. George Steiner for one), is another distorted form of FAITH, able to inspire martyrdom in millions. Substituting the traditional values of the Judeo-Christian heritage with this Marxist-Satanic faith is one of the basic principles of subversion at the stage of DEMORALIZATION — the highest and most effective level of IDEAS. The methods are as primitive as they are predictable. You do not have to be a graduate of a KGB school or Harvard University to figure out what kind of INTERACTION between the subverter (KGB) and target (American brains) occurs on this level.

All the SUBVERTER — be it Andropov's KGB or any other purposeful group or organization hell-bent on the idea of a "New World Order"— must do is to study the areas where your nation's IDEAS could be eroded and substituted, and then slowly but consistently affect these areas by sending infiltrating Agents of Influence to inject new ideas, disseminate propagandist literature, and encourage self-destructive tendencies.

All a subverter must do to remove the spiritual backbone of America is to help you to POLITICIZE, COMMERCIALIZE and 'ENTERTAINMENTALIZE' the dominant religions. There are many other contributing factors the subverter can also take advantage of, such as the development and spreading of various religious cults, including Satanic and Death cults; preaching moral relativity and removing religion (and prayer, ANY prayer) from schools; creating 'personality cults' in religion whereby the preacher becomes the center and object of divine worship, not God (often your religious charlatans claim to be 'incarnations' of God, or even God Himself), etc.

I have selected the above three main methods because I am most familiar with them. These methods were used by myself and my KGB-Novosti colleagues and these methods have proven to be sufficiently efficient. We did not have to bother with such silliness for example as recruiting Billy Graham and forcing him to tell outrageous lies about "the existence of religious freedom in the Soviet Union" in state-run churches in Moscow.

Let's start with the most 'innocent' method of destroying religion, namely, making it ENTERTAINING. To attract people

LOVE LETTER TO AMERICA

AND MONEY to 'established' religious organizations some churches have literally become theaters conducting variety shows featuring celebrities from the entertainment 'industry' who perform for 'fees'. The KGB Agents of Influence may or may not have to physically manipulate these entertainment arrangements. The indiscriminate choice of the 'celebrities' for these church 'performances' is usually quite pleasing to the KGB. A group of rock or pop-musicians with a message of 'social-justice' sugar-coated in popular 'spiritual' tunes can be more helpful to the KGB than someone standing in the pulpit preaching Marxist-Leninist doctrine. The sugar-sweet messages of social equality from the crooning mouths of the entertainers are quite enough to accomplish the aims of the KGB without any overt activity on their part.

COMMERCIALIZATION of religion does the same thing. If the church must SOLICIT your money and remind you repeatedly in every TV show to contribute (with telephone numbers to pledge donations), that only means and infers that there is something basically wrong with your faith. Faithful people do not have to be ASKED for money, they tithe to their churches voluntarily and eagerly. Unhealthy competition for donations between various 'electronic churches' does two things beneficial to the subverter (KGB):

1) It makes religion dependent on the most successful 'salesmen' of God (and these salesmen may not necessarily

be of the highest moral standards, nor must they be) thus, truly moral, God -centered people are turned off by organized religion and 2) it EMPTIES regular churches, where you practice your religion by personal physical presence and participation and involvement. All the subverter must do now is to keep on further discrediting the main body of the church, by harping at religion in general as "just another means of the capitalist exploitation of masses, and a profit-oriented opiate of the people". And the Soviet propaganda, and its fronts such as 'Novosti' Press Agency does exactly that, and quite successfully, through thousands of 'liberal' and 'leftist' media establishments in the USA.

Politicizing religion is the most efficient method of demoralizing a target nation. Once a nation starts giving to Caesar what belongs to God, and getting God involved in such things as 'social justice' and partisan political squabbles, it predictably loses what religion calls mercy and the grace of God. To put it in 'atheistic' terms, a target country allows the subverter to use the area of moral values for dissemination and enforcement of amoral ideas and policies. The most powerful instrument of this process is an organization called World Council of Churches, infiltrated by the KGB to such extent, that it is hard to distinguish, these days, a priest from a spy. Being a public relations officer for Novosti, I accompanied many foreign members of the WCC during their visits to the USSR. Some of them struck me as individuals pathologically unable to say or hear truth. They were simply allergic to any facts or opinions which would 'undermine' their 'spiritual' affiliation with the Soviet manipulators. Archbishop and President (!) Macarios of Cyprus was one such 'religious' visitor.

Skillfully combining both God's and Caesar's things, Macarios was extremely effective in bringing the desperately needed air of legitimacy and 'holiness' to the junta of the Soviet mass murderers and oppressors of religion. His photogenic presence at various 'international forums' in Moscow greatly promoted ACCEPTABILITY of the Soviet influence in the 'non-aligned' and 'developing' countries.

When, after my defection to the West, I find Trotskyite publications in a United Church of Canada, or see Nicaraguan Catholic Church 'fathers' with Soviet-made Kalashnikov machine guns hung over their church robes, or read about 'humanitarian' aid from the American Council of Churches given to African mass-murderers and terrorists, who were trained in my old country by the KGB, I do not 'suspect' I KNOW these things to be what they are — direct results of the Communist SUBVERSION of religion. I do not need any 'evidence' of 'links' between the KGB and the church. The complete confusion of God-related and politically subverted related goals is obvious.

In the extreme left column of my chart, you can see the

TOMAS SCHUMAN

RESULTS of DEMORALIZATION in each individual area on each level of subversion. The result of the demoralization of religion is a phenomenon referred to as the "death wish". This expression is borrowed from a book by a Soviet dissident writer, Igor Shafarevich, entitled *Socialism as a Historical Phenomenon*. (YMCA Press, Paris, 1977) Dr. Shafarevich in analyzing the 'dead' civilizations of Egypt, Maya, Mohenjo-Dara, Babylon, etc., comes to an ominous conclusion:

EVERY ONE OF THESE CIVILIZATIONS DIED WHEN PEOPLE REJECTED RELIGION AND GOD AND TRIED TO CREATE 'SOCIAL JUSTICE' ALONG THE SOCIALIST PRINCIPLES.

Thus, Socialism, according to Shafarevich, may be a manifestation of an inborn human instinct of SELF-DESTRUCTION, if unrestrained — leading ultimately to PHYSICAL DEATH OF ALL MANKIND.

'MASS' EDUCATION

This is another area of subversion at the stage of demoralization.

The Marxist-Leninist concept of education emphasizes 'environment' and 'mass' character of education over individual abilities and quality. When American media enthusiastically reports (repeating Soviet propaganda cliches) about 'achievements of Soviet science', they usually obscure the IDEOLOGICAL aspects and purposes of the Communist system of education. 'Massiveness' and 'universality' of education attracts Western sociologists and governmental bureaucracies alike. For the 'developing' nations this seems to be the easiest short-cut to many contemporary problems.

The Western public seldom receives the explanation of THE PRICE of the state-controlled Socialist-type education: political conformity to dictatorship, ideological brainwashing, lack of individual initiative in 'educated masses', lagging in development of science and technology. It is a commonly known fact that most of the Soviet 'technological marvels' are stolen, bought, or 'borrowed' from the West. Most of the scientific and technological research in the USSR is 'productive' only and always in the most destructive area: the military. My motherland is still, after more than half century of 'victorious Socialism', a country without even common household refrigerators, and yet boasts of their 'space exploration' and tremendous military might, which have done absolutely nothing to improve the day-to-day life of Soviet citizens.

The American romance with state-run education as encouraged by KGB subverters has already produced generations of graduates who cannot spell, cannot find Nicaragua on a world map, cannot THINK creatively and independently. I wonder if Albert Einstein would have arrived at his Theory of Relativity if he had been educated in one of today's American public schools. Most likely he would have 'discovered' marijuana and variant methods of sexual intercourse instead.

Wouldn't you agree that KGB sponsored demoralization is no? going to produce the dynamic, talented, and fruitful young Americans of the future? Contemporary American permissiveness and moral relativity in education have greatly facilitated Soviet ideological subversion tactics.

The main methods of Soviet DEMORALIZATION of American education are:

1. Student Exchanges whereby American students and professors go to Moscow and are exposed to ideological brainwashing sometimes lacking the proper education that would allow them to assess the Soviet information they receive objectively;

2. Flooding of campus bookstores with Marxist and Socialist literature published both in the USSR and by domestic 'fellow travelers';

3. International seminars and conferences with Soviet participation, where Soviet propaganda seldom is balanced by opposing viewpoints;

LOVE LETTER TO AMERICA

4. Infiltration of schools and universities by radicals, leftists, and simply 'disturbers', often functioning unknowingly under the direct guidance of KGB Agents of Influence;

5. Establishing numerous 'student' newspapers and magazines, staffed with Communists and sympathizers;

6. Organizing 'study groups' and 'circles' for dissemination of Soviet propaganda and Communist ideology;

The eventual result is very predictable: ignorance combined with anti-Americanism. That's good enough for the KGB at this stage of subversion.

LORDS OF PUBLIC OPINION

The American media is a willing recipient of Soviet subversion. I know this, because I worked with American journalists and correspondents in Moscow while on the Soviet side, and after my defection to the West. People habitually refer to the American media as 'free', ignoring the obvious and commonly known fact that most of the most powerful media in the USA, is already MONOPOLIZED both financially and ideologically by what are referred to as 'liberals'.

American media 'chains' BELONG to fewer and fewer owners, who, do not seem to mind that the media is being almost totally 'liberalized'. Liberalism, in its old classical sense, means above all, respect to individual opinion and tolerance to opposing views.

However, in my own experience, communist defectors who have requested and sometimes literally begged, to have stories of their life in the Soviet Union told to the American people via the major American media have been completely ignored.

Tomas Schuman with a copy of 'Look" magazine he helped to produce as a Novosti manipulator.

LOVE LETTER TO AMERICA

Look's idea of 'Russian fashions' inspired by Novosti manipulators. 'All is fine in Soviet Russia after 50 years of Communism' - that was the message.

Propaganda monument in Volgograd as presented by the 'Look" magazine.

Schuman (center) with group of American guests, including Look's photographer Phillip Harrington, who took the pictures for the propaganda issue of Look magazine.

One of the most devastating methods of Soviet subversion in American media is the DISCREDITING of authors like me and the information and opinion of those who come up with clear evidence of Communist crimes against mankind. This method is well described in my forthcoming book entirely dedicated to the activity of the 'Novosti' Press Agency.

Introduction of NON-ISSUES is another powerful method of demoralizing at the level of IDEAS. It will take another full-size book to describe in detail this method. Suffice it will be here to give a brief definition of NON-ISSUES. An issue, the solution of which creates more and bigger problems for majority of a nation, even though it may benefit a few, is a non-issue (civil rights of homosexuals is not an issue; defending sexual morality is the larger, real issue).

The main purpose of non-issues and the devastating result of their introduction is the SIDE-TRACKING of public opinion, energy (both mental and physical), money and TIME from the constructive solutions. Soviet propaganda elevated the art of infiltrating and emphasizing non-issues in American public life to the level of actual state policy.

ADDICTIVE 'MASS CULTURE'

Years ago, when I was scanning through a pile of Western newspapers in Novosti's Moscow headquarters, I came across a column written by a Canadian writer, Gregory Clark in the *Toronto Star*.

Here it is in full. I have saved it for my files; "If I were a Communist agent in America with millions of dollars to spend annually, I would not waste it in bribing public servants to give away state secrets. But I would lavish and encourage the sleazy tunesmiths of that region to turn out more and more garbage 'culture' . . . Gaggled-headed and obscure musicians would be helped to prominence. I would seek out the more questionable publishers of the dirtier paperbacks and slip them a few hundred thousand so they could set up more respectable head offices. Wherever trend shows towards the beat generation I would offer it a helping hand. Anything that prompted the insubordination of teenagers, anything that contributes to the confusion and exasperation of parents would be most liberally endowed. The basic intention of my spending would be to break down the discipline, encourage relaxation of authority of every kind to build up, in as short time as possible, an adult generation that could easily go out of control.

A typical 'press conference' at the Indian Embassy in Moscow. At least half of the 'journalists' are KGB agents. Indian Ambassador Kewal Singh (1) probably did not mind. Tomas Schuman (4) does his job as a Novosti-KBG agent.

America would look desperately around for any kind of discipline to rescue them and THERE — would be Communism, the most iron-fisted discipline since Sparta. The victory would be bloodless . . . Except of course in concentration camps, torture, prisons, and few things like that. . .

LOVE LETTER TO AMERICA

But nobody would know about that because of censorship of the press."

This was written in 1959! The accuracy of this description oi OUR activity stunned me. We had just completed 'helping a gaggle-headed' Communist entertainer, Yves Montand to 'prominence' in Moscow and were halfway through with publicly elevating 'obscure' Indian filmmaker — Raj Kapoor to 'fame'. The editorial offices of Novosti were teaming with 'sleazy' foreign singers, poets, writers, artists, musicians, and 'intellectuals' coming to my country for support in their 'progressive struggle' against their own 'decadent capitalist' societies ...

There is not much I can add to that statement of a wise Canadian columnist today. Yes, KGB encourages DEMORALIZATION of America through the 'mass culture' by relying upon the help of the "useful idiots" of the entertainment business. No, the Beatles, Punks and Michael Jackson are not on the KGB payroll. They are on YOUR payroll. All the KGB had to do is to CHANGE YOUR ATTITUDES and kill your RESISTANCE to the demoralizing addiction your kids call 'music', make it acceptable, NORMAL; make it a part of 'American culture' where it does not belong and never did slowly and gradually.

THE SECOND LEVEL OF DEMORALIZATION: STRUCTURES

There is a Russian proverb which says: "The sly head gives no rest to the arms". Let us see what Communist subversion does to your "arms" — the socio/ political/ economical STRUCTURES of America. The areas of application for demoralizing American structures are:

1. Judicial and Law-enforcement system;

2. Public organizations and institutions dealing with RELATIONS between individuals, groups, and classes of the society;

3. Security and defense organs;

4. Internal political parties and groups;

5. Foreign policy formulating bodies both governmental and non-governmental ("think-tanks", academia, "Sovietology advisors" etc.);

In the area of "Law and Order", the method of demoralization is to promote and enforce the prevalence of the "legalistic" approach over the "moral" one. Several generations of American lawyers and lawmakers, graduating from the 'liberal' (that is LEFTIST, Socialist-oriented) schools, after long-time exposure to the Socialist IDEOLOGY, have already created an atmosphere in the U.S. judicial system whereby "underprivileged" criminals are treated as a "victims" of the "cruel American society", and the real victim (the law-abiding society) is turned into defenseless and very underprivileged citizens and taxpayers, PAYING for a comparatively comfortable life of the criminal in or outside prison. The result is as predictable as it is desirable for the subverter: MISTRUST of the American population towards their own judicial and law-enforcement system, and people demanding harsher punishments and stricter CONTROLS to fight crime. And what could be better than Soviet or Communist-type control? Even your 'liberal' media claims that there is no street crime in Moscow and no drug problem in the USSR.

Similarly, in social life, by encouraging you to put your individual RIGHTS over your OBLIGATIONS (any obligations — private, financial, moral, patriotic etc.) the subverter achieves the desired effect: a society composed of IRRESPONSIBLE INDIVIDUALS, each one "doing his own thing", and acting according to the "law of jungle". Such subversion of society is the first step to tyranny.

To demoralize America's PROTECTIVE FORCES, it is enough to make your kids call the police "pigs" and "fascists" for a decade, disband police agencies watching over subverters and radicals by calling them "spies" (that is exactly what American Union of Civil Liberties did), stage campaign after campaign of discreditation and "investigation" of the wrongdoings" of the police, and in 20 years you arrive at the present situation, when the majority of civilian population of this nation is virtually without civil laws or protection from murderers, lunatics, criminals, etc. Can you now expect your police and civil authorities to protect you and your family in case of terrorist attack or a major civil disturbance?

The American FBI and CIA have had no better treatment. Americans are MADE to believe that your own security agencies pose more danger than the Soviet KGB. There were dozens of "revelations" and exposes on the CIA during the last 10 to 15 years. But there was not a SINGLE public trial of any Soviet agent of the KGB caught in the USA "red-handed". There were numerous expulsions of Soviet 'diplomats' yes. But an equal or greater number of them came to America to replace their 'fallen comrades'.

There is not a SINGLE law in America which could be used to legally persecute KGB agents for ideological subversion. But there is a law that prevents your CIA from using YOUR media to vindicate their acts to protect YOU against the KGB subversion. Your media and your Hollywood entertainers lovingly repeat every fabrication of Soviet propaganda regarding the CIA 'atrocities', mixing it with truth, half-truth, and blatant lie. Demoralizers like Larry Flint regularly entertain the public with juicy stories about 'CIA assassinations'

LOVE LETTER TO AMERICA

sandwiched between pornographic pictures in his magazine. Do you remember when you saw an American film or read a book about the 'good CIA"? I do not imply that pornographer Flint or members of Rockefeller commission on CIA are on the KGB payroll. But obviously pornography, as well as political prostitution pays. It sells 'Hustler' magazine. It sells politicians . . . and it kills the security of America. Criticism of the KGB does not pay. In fact, critics of KGB subverters may get killed in the process. What are you, my dear Americans? A nation of masochists and cowards? When you read and listen to all this dirt poured upon your security agencies by the media and politicians, can't you realize, that the most just and factual criticism of the CIA is wrongly addressed? Security agencies of America (unlike the KGB) are INSTRUMENTS in the hands of a nation and her elected POLITICIANS. One should not blame an instrument, when it is the OPERATOR'S fault. If the instrument malfunctions — CORRECT it, and don't use a hammer where a fine screwdriver is needed.

Very often American media presents a picture of CIA and FBI as a 'mirror reflection' of the KGB and its 'fraternal services'. False. The KGB is a POWER which systematically and ruthlessly MURDERED about SIXTY MILLION of my countrymen, and still engages in the killing of innocent defenseless people all over the world. How many were killed by the CIA? Do numbers (and 'quality') matter at all to you?

TOMAS SCHUMAN

Or was Comrade Stalin right, when he said that ONE person shot is a tragedy, but one MILLION a statistic?

Now let's look at how you treat your military. What is the image of the military presented to you and the rest of the world in the American press and the electronic media? If there is a U.S. general, he is called a trigger-happy 'warmonger', a 'hawk' and 'aggressor'. One of the most popular TV series — M.A.S.H. — presents your military as a bunch of very humorous, hysterically funny bunch of psychotics, queers, alcoholics, and otherwise rather unruly characters. Recently I saw a film titled "Rage", where the Pentagon is depicted as a cruel experimenter, testing chemical weapons on unsuspecting American farmers. And it is shown on TV exactly at the very same time when Soviets are using chemical weapons in Afghanistan, Cambodia, and Laos, and provide the same to their Iraqi 'brothers' for their fraternal genocide in Persian Gulf. Have you EVER seen a movie or a TV series about THAT? Every American student knows the name of the Vietnamese village Mi-Lai and what it stands for, namely, an "American war crime." Do you remember the name of the Soviet pilot who shot down the Korean passenger airliner with 269 passengers aboard, including some 60 Americans and a US senator? Do you remember the name of that senator? Does anybody in America EVER learn from American media the names of thousands of Cambodian and Afghani villages TOTALLY

LOVE LETTER TO AMERICA

EXTERMINATED by the Soviet military? Where is Jane Fonda and Dr. Spock, who used to express so much concern and love for Vietnamese and Cambodians when the US military was there?

The 'double standard' applied and enforced and LEGITIMIZED by the manipulators of public opinion in the USA is a direct result of the long-term process of the DEMORALIZATION of the IMAGE of the US MILITARY in the minds of millions all over the world.

The result? Study the chart . . .

'Quiet Diplomacy' or surrender?

There are hundreds of volumes written about the ways Communists use foreign relations for their purposes. There are NONE which reveal the link between the failures of American diplomacy and the process of demoralization. From time-to-time defectors from the Communist side, such as Arkady Shevchenko, the USSR representative in the UN, give breath-taking accounts on how the Communists are using 'diplomacy' for subversion. And yet all the crowds of "experts" and "Kremlinologists" are seemingly unable to put the pieces together and to raise their voices AGAINST dealing with the Communists in a 'diplomatic' way.

Many public figures have noted that most of Americans do

not want to hear unpleasant things. Politicians in the USA know this. So does the KGB. Every American administration has contributed to the process of DEMORALIZATION of their own foreign policy by continuously negotiating and SIGNING "peace treaties" From the "Lend Lease" to the "Helsinki Accord" to the "SALT" treaties, creating false expectations and voter complacency and NEVER openly and honestly admitting that NONE of those agreements and treaties EVER WOR KED — for America that is — They ALL benefited the USSR, however. In the process America has lost MOST of her foreign friends to the 'Socialist camp' — Concentration camp, to be precise. Presently the USA is rapidly nearing a situation of TOTAL ISOLATION from the rest of the world. Even our long-time friend Great Britain did not support America, even verbally, on the liberation of Grenada, despite the obvious fact that America was on the British side in the ridiculous war over the Falkland Islands.

What could be more amoral than the 'peace with honor' signed by Kissinger with Hanoi Communists? — ask the Vietnamese 'boat people'. When someone makes a deal with a murderer, we call him 'accomplice in crime', we don't award him with 'Nobel Peace Prize'.

Or do we? What should we call this kind of foreign policy which is both amoral AND hurts America?

LEVEL THREE: UNHEALTHY BODY — UNHEALTHY MIND

Demoralization in such areas as family life, health services, interracial relations, population control and distribution and labor relations I call the 'LIFE' level.

Marxist-Leninist ideology coated in various indigenous "social theories" have greatly contributed to the process of American family break-up. The trend recently is changing in the opposite direction, but many generations of Americans, brought up in broken families, are already adults lacking one of the most vital qualities for the survival of a nation — LOYALTY. A child who has not learned to be loyal to his family will hardly make a loyal citizen. Such child may grow into adult who is loyal to the State though. The USSR example is rather revealing in this case. In the struggle for the 'final victory of Communism', the goal of the subverter is to substitute, as slowly and painlessly as possible, the concept of loyalty for NATION with loyalty to the "Big Brother" welfare state, who gives everything and can TAKE everything, including personal freedom — from every citizen. If that objective is successfully achieved, the subverter does not need any nuclear warheads and tanks and may not even need the physical military INVASION. All that is needed is the 'election' of a 'progressive thinking' President who will be voted to power by Americans, who have been addicted to welfare and 'security' as defined by Soviet subverters.

TOMAS SCHUMAN

Remarkably similar methods are being used in medical and health services and sports, (as part of an activity meant to keep the population healthy). By encouraging 'professionalism' in spectator sports ' rather than encouraging individual sports participation, America enfeebles herself as a nation. Most American adults who 'love sports' watch TV sports programs, while munching pretzels with their beer, and NOT taking physical participation in sports activity. Unlike in the USSR, sports are not a COMPULSORY part of elementary education in America. Impressive victories of Soviet athletes at international competitions further facilitate the IDEAS OF THE SUPREMACY of SOCIALISM in public health, thus convincing more and more Americans of the need to emulate the Soviet system and introduce it into the American schools.

What many Americans do not realize, is that what they see on their TV screens is not REAL Soviet sport. Most of the USSR population is not 'athletic' at all; they are sick from the lack of correct nutrition and alcoholism. Soviet athletes are state-created exceptions to the general national deterioration in the USSR.

A similar myth is being promoted in the U.S. about 'free health care' in the USSR. While working in Moscow, accompanying numerous foreign delegations, and showing them 'regular' medical facilities in clinics and kolkhos

LOVE LETTER TO AMERICA

hospitals my guests did not all realize that I was taking them to specially prepared 'exclusive' medical establishments, 'only for the eyes of foreigners'. When I arranged interviews with Soviet doctors, telling my guests about the 'glorious achievements' of Soviet surgery, some of them had no way of checking if these 'achievements' were available to USSR collective farmers or workers in Siberia. They are not. And many Americans know about this, although they have never visited my old country. Yet the tendency of U.S. bureaucrats is to enlarge the state-run Medicare, even though, as shown in the USSR and elsewhere, socialized medicine is substandard, less efficient, and most definitely less progressive than privately owned and operated medical facilities within a properly functioning free market system.

Demoralization in food CONSUMPTION patterns is also effective in the introduction of such things as 'junk foods'. No, KGB agents do not put chemicals into American food and drink. It is done by some American mega-monopolies who operate along the same principles as Soviet 'Obshchepit' (Public Food Service): they look at consumers as 'units of consumers', not individuals. Abolishing freely competing SMALL food companies, who HAD TO TREAT YOU INDIVIDUALLY to survive economically, these giants of indigestion artificially CREATE consumers' tastes and demands which may not be in the interests of your health but surely in the interests of the monopoly profit. And here I tend to agree, at least in part, with America's Ralph Nader, and consumer protection groups, although I do not share their ideas on the solution of the problem racial and ethnic interrelations is one of the most vulnerable areas for demoralization. There is not a single Communist country where racial groups are 'equal' and enjoy as much freedom to develop themselves culturally and economically as in America. There are not too many "Capitalists" countries where ethnic minorities have it as good as in the U S A. I have been to many countries of the world and I can state to you, my dear Americans, that your society is the least discriminatory. The Communist 'solution' for racial problem is 'final': they simply murder those who are different AND stubbornly insist on remaining different. Stalin played with whole populations of 'ethnics' — 'resettling' Estonians, Latvians, and Lithuanians in Siberia, relocating Crimean Tartars from the tropics to permafrost and Koreans from the Far East to the Kazakhstan deserts. But unfortunately, an 'average' American never recalls these commonly known facts when his attention is drawn to domestic 'racial discrimination' issues by those who profess 'racial harmony' along the socialist guidelines. Why? Simple: because American 'race discrimination fighters' NEVER MENTION these facts. If the USA were located on a separate planet from the Communists, I would probably agree with Martin Luther King when he said that "America is a racist country'. But when

LOVE LETTER TO AMERICA

these statements are made on TH IS planet and in THE MOST INTEGRATED NATION IN THE WORLD, I say to your 'fighters for racial equality': you are hypocrites and instruments (even if unwilling) of DEMORALIZATION.

The American traditional solution of racial and ethnic problems is slow but efficient: the 'melting pot' which raises the less developed groups to a HIGHER level. It has worked for more than a century of American history and created the most harmonious and productive nation on Earth. The present day 'solution' to racial inequality is borrowed from Communist mythology: EQUALITY of all racial and ethnic groups LEGISLATED by the government and ENFORCED by state bureaucracies. We know perfectly well that neither races nor INDIVIDUALS are equal, in every respect. We know that every nation and race has a peculiar character, abilities, traditions, mentality, and ability to learn and its individual PACE OF DEVELOPMENT. By mimicking the Soviet 'national policy' of equality America simply erases the distinct racial characteristics that have made this country great.

Very briefly on population distribution: urbanization and "delandization" (the taking away of private land) is the greatest threat to American nationhood. Why? Because the poor farmer often is a greater PATRIOT than an affluent dweller of a large congested American city. Communists know this very well. The Soviets keep a very tight control over the size of their cities by the system of 'police registration of residence' called 'propiska'. They know perfectly well that the farmer will fight an invader until last bullet ON HIS LAND.

"Underprivileged" or urbanized masses on the other hand, may feel like meeting an invader with flowers and red banners. ALIENATION of people from privately-owned land is one of the particularly important methods of DEMORALIZATION.

And, finally, we have come to the last, but not least, important area: labor relations. I do not think I have to tell you about ideological infiltration of some labor unions in the USA. This is a well-documented part of your history. Moscow 'International Trade-Union School', a KGB incubator for agents, takes care of physical infiltration of labor unions. And that is also well known (even to the CIA) in fact.

What I want you to think about today is what sort of MORALITY it takes to make medical nurses leave sick and dying patients in hospital beds and walk out to strike for fifty cents an hour more in pay? OK, for a full DOLLAR more? What makes unionized electricians leave a city without power in the middle of a severe winter and let several children in "under privileged" slums freeze to DEATH? How desperate for money must a unionized truck driver be to SHOOT TO DEATH a strike-breaking colleague, father of five?

LOVE LETTER TO AMERICA

Surely, each individual American, who commits these outrageously AMORAL acts is not that cruel and egocentric. And, let's face it, not THAT broke. So, why? My answer is — IDEOLOGICAL DEMORALIZATION.

The bargaining process in American labor in many instances is no longer motivated by the desire to IMPROVE working conditions and wages. In many cases it is not bargaining at all — it is blackmail.

And in the process of the unlimited growth of union POWER, the American worker loses the only relevant and real freedom he has in this country: the freedom to choose, to work or not to work, and for how much. If an individual prefers to work for LOWER pay (and it must be his free individual choice), he often is no longer able to do so.

I have just mentioned what happens to strike-breakers in America.

STAGE TWO: DESTABILIZATION

Here the efforts of subverter narrow down to the "essentials": the internal power structures of a target nation; the nation's foreign relations; economy and "social fiber". If the preceding stage of DEMORALIZATION is successful, the subverter is no longer concerned about your IDEAS and your LIFE. Now he gets to the 'spinal cord' of your country and helps YOU to bring your own society into the state of DESTABILIZATION. That may take from 2 to 5 years, depending on the maturity of a nation and its ability to mobilize for resistance.

POWER STRUGGLE

The first symptom of instability is expressed as the desire of the population to bring to power those politicians and parties who are charismatic, act like good "caretakers" and promise more "security" — not from external and foreign enemies, but rather, job "security", "free" social services and other "pleasure strokes" provided by "Big Brother". By concentrating the attention of a nation on short-term solutions and "improvements", such irresponsible politicians simply procrastinate on facing "the moment of truth", when the nation will have to pay a much higher price for the main and basic problem — bringing country back to stability and restoring the moral fiber.

A compounding factor at this stage is the so-called "grass root" participation of the 'masses' in the political process. Demoralized and enfeebled 'masses' tend to grab the 'easiest' short-cut solution to social ills and socialism seems to them to be the best answer. Traditional national institutions no longer appear efficient. They are gradually replaced by artificially created 'citizen's committees' and 'boards' which acquire more and more political power. These bodies which are in essence, mirror reflections of the totalitarian structures of power, are more and more 'responsive' to mobocracy, the rule of the crowd of radicalized CONSUMERS. At the same time, the backbone of the economy — the free bargaining process — gradually yields to the principle of 'planned economy' and 'centralization'.

With the final destruction of the free bargaining process the predominant economic power moves into the hands of "Big Brother", the State, which functions more and more 'in cahoots' with mega-monopolies and monopolized labor unions. The famous 'division of powers' no longer governs the judicial, legislative, and executive lines, but rather is replaced by bureaucracy in government, bureaucracy in business and bureaucracy in labor.

In the area of foreign relations America is being pushed further and further into isolationism and defeatism. Few remaining friends look with horror at the destiny of those nations who were betrayed and abandoned by the USA and try to find 'their own solutions', which often comes as 'establishing friendly relations' with the USSR and its Communist empire. The belligerent encirclement of America proceeds with an ever-increasing pace and demoralized politicians are no longer able or willing to face the inevitable reality. Soviet and Cuban military supplies and direct intervention seem to the U S legislators to be less dangerous, than America's 'losing face' by 'violating international laws' by mining Nicaraguan ports to prevent the export of Communist revolution to the region. Most Americans are made to believe that it is their country — America — who 'violates' international law, not the USSR and its surrogates. The average American may not even realize that the 'International Court' is nothing but an artificial creature of the Soviet-controlled General Assembly of the UN.

All through this stage of DESTABILIZATION, Western 'multi-national' monopolies continue to trade, extend credits, supply technology and 'diplomatically' appease the SUBVERTER — the Central Committee of the USSR. In total disregard of the interests of the peoples of America and the USSR, these two giants continue to extend aid to each other. American media keeps talking about 'frictions' between the NATIONS (USA— USSR)! What 'frictions'?

Comrade Pertov in Omsk has NO FRICTIONS with Mr. Smith in Pittsburg. In fact, they never had a chance to meet each other thanks to Helsinki Accord. Comrade Petrov, though HAS FRICTIONS with his oppressors — the Kremlin junta, which sends him to make war on Afghanistan, Vietnam, Angola, and Nicaragua. Comrade Petrov does not want war with America. Neither does Mr. Smith want to fight 'Russia'. But they may have to if the DESTABILIZATION process is successful in America. Once it is, the situation inevitably slides into . . .

STAGE THREE: CRISIS

It may take only 2 to 6 months, to bring America to the same situation which now exists South of the border in Central America.

At this third stage of subversion, you will have all your American 'radicals' and Soviet 'sleeper' agents springing into action, trying to 'seize power as quickly and ruthlessly as possible" (see the 'Rules of Revolution' in the beginning of this booklet). If all the previous stages of Soviet subversion have been successfully completed by that time, most Americans will be so totally confused that they may even WELCOME some "strong' leaders who 'know how to talk to the Russians'. Chances are these leaders will be elected and given almost unlimited 'emergency powers'. A forceful change of the U.S. system may or may not be accomplished through a civil war or internal revolution, and a physical MILITARY invasion by the USSR may not even have to take place at all. But change it will be, and rather a drastic one, with all the familiar attributes of Soviet 'progress' being instituted such as NATIONALIZATION of vital industries, the reduction of the 'private sector' of the economy to the bare minimum, the redistribution of wealth and a massive propaganda campaign by the newly 'elected' government to 'explain' and justify the reforms.

TOMAS SCHUMAN

No — no concentration camps and executions. Not yet. That will come later at the stage of . . .

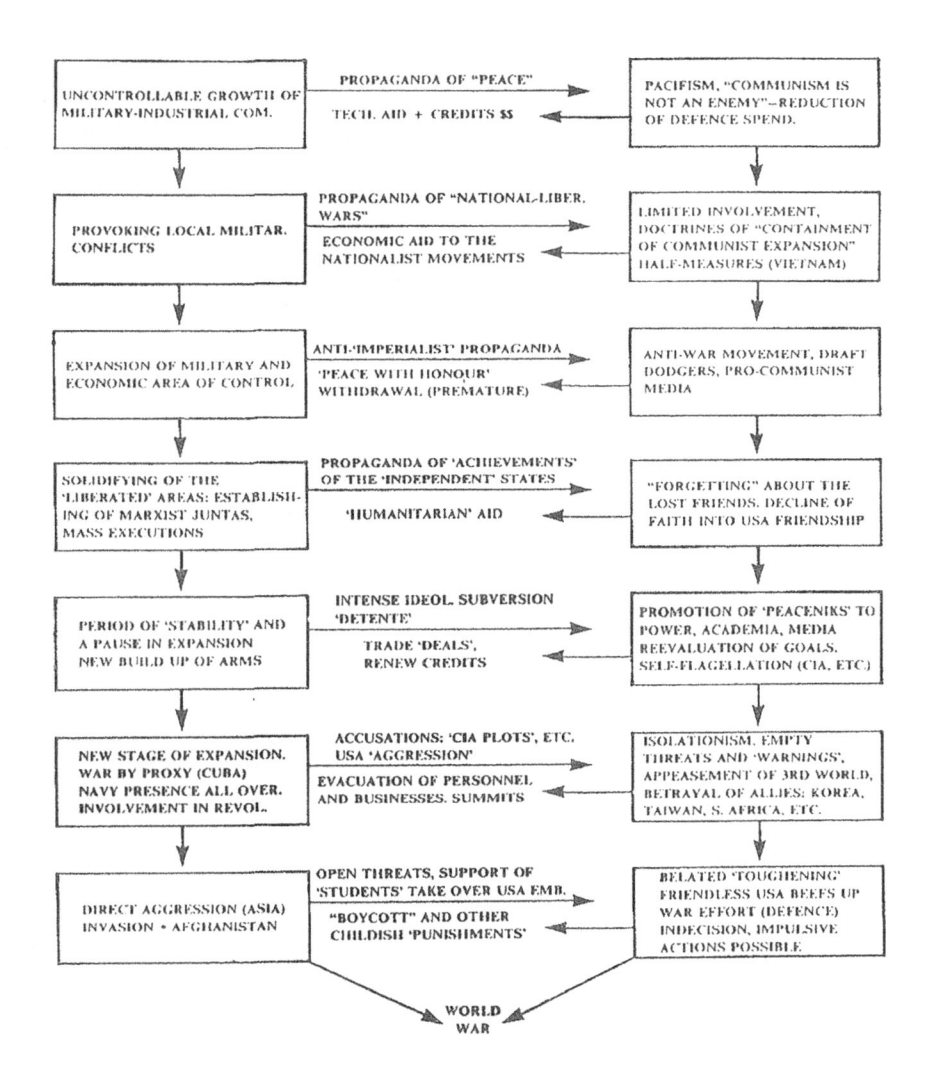

SUBVERTER ACTIONS	PROPAGANDA / DIPLOMATIC	TARGET NATION RESPONSE
UNCONTROLLABLE GROWTH OF MILITARY-INDUSTRIAL COM.	PROPAGANDA OF "PEACE" → ← TECH. AID + CREDITS $$	PACIFISM, "COMMUNISM IS NOT AN ENEMY"—REDUCTION OF DEFENCE SPEND.
PROVOKING LOCAL MILITAR. CONFLICTS	PROPAGANDA OF "NATIONAL-LIBER. WARS" → ← ECONOMIC AID TO THE NATIONALIST MOVEMENTS	LIMITED INVOLVEMENT, DOCTRINES OF "CONTAINMENT OF COMMUNIST EXPANSION" HALF-MEASURES (VIETNAM)
EXPANSION OF MILITARY AND ECONOMIC AREA OF CONTROL	ANTI-'IMPERIALIST' PROPAGANDA → ← 'PEACE WITH HONOUR' WITHDRAWAL (PREMATURE)	ANTI-WAR MOVEMENT, DRAFT DODGERS, PRO-COMMUNIST MEDIA
SOLIDIFYING OF THE 'LIBERATED' AREAS: ESTABLISH- ING OF MARXIST JUNTAS, MASS EXECUTIONS	PROPAGANDA OF 'ACHIEVEMENTS' OF THE 'INDEPENDENT' STATES → ← 'HUMANITARIAN' AID	"FORGETTING" ABOUT THE LOST FRIENDS. DECLINE OF FAITH INTO USA FRIENDSHIP
PERIOD OF 'STABILITY' AND A PAUSE IN EXPANSION NEW BUILD UP OF ARMS	INTENSE IDEOL. SUBVERSION 'DETENTE' → ← TRADE 'DEALS', RENEW CREDITS	PROMOTION OF 'PEACENIKS' TO POWER, ACADEMIA, MEDIA REEVALUATION OF GOALS. SELF-FLAGELLATION (CIA, ETC.)
NEW STAGE OF EXPANSION. WAR BY PROXY (CUBA) NAVY PRESENCE ALL OVER. INVOLVEMENT IN REVOL..	ACCUSATIONS: 'CIA PLOTS', ETC. USA 'AGGRESSION' → ← EVACUATION OF PERSONNEL AND BUSINESSES. SUMMITS	ISOLATIONISM. EMPTY THREATS AND 'WARNINGS', APPEASEMENT OF 3RD WORLD, BETRAYAL OF ALLIES: KOREA, TAIWAN, S. AFRICA, ETC.
DIRECT AGGRESSION (ASIA) INVASION - AFGHANISTAN	OPEN THREATS, SUPPORT OF 'STUDENTS' TAKE OVER USA EMB. → ← "BOYCOTT" AND OTHER CHILDISH 'PUNISHMENTS'	BELATED 'TOUGHENING' FRIENDLESS USA BEEFS UP WAR EFFORT (DEFENCE) INDECISION, IMPULSIVE ACTIONS POSSIBLE

→ WORLD WAR ←

This chart explains in detail the steps in the subversion process from the destabilization stage to the crisis stage (see chart of "The Subversion Process" in the areas of economics, military, and diplomatic relations. The longer arrow the response of the target nation to the actions of the subverter.

NORMALIZATION: THE FOURTH AND LAST STAGE

Any normal nation would resist such a 'progressive change'. As I have just described. And according to the 'classics of Marxism-Leninism' there will arise pockets of resistance, shortly after the takeover consisting of the 'enemy classes and counter-revolutionaries' who will physically resist the new system. Some Americans may take to arms and flee to the mountains (as in Afghanistan). Reforms (or DESTRUCTION to be more accurate) of the security agencies, (police and military) by the new government may lead to a situation of 'split loyalties' among law enforcement officers and render most of the population defenseless. At this point, to avoid 'the bloodshed', the subverter moves to NORMALIZATION, a term borrowed from the Soviet propaganda of 1968 — from the time of the Soviet 'fraternal' invasion of Czechoslovakia. Comrade Brezhnev called that 'NORMALIZATION'. And he was right: the vanquished country was brought BY FORCE into the NORMAL state of SOCIALISM: namely, subjugation.

This is when my dear friends, you will start seeing 'friendly' Soviet soldiers in the streets of our cities working together with American soldiers and the 'new' police force to 'restore law and order'. Very soon your yesterday's American socialist radicals and 'do-gooders who were working so hard to bring 'progress' to their own country will find themselves IN PRISONS and hastily built concentration camps. Many of them will be

EXECUTED, quietly or publicly. Why? Simple: The Soviet 'liberators' will have no further use for the 'disturbers'. The 'useful idiots' will have completed their work. From then on, the New Order will need STABILITY and NEW MORALITY. No more 'grass roots' movements. No more criticism of the State. The Press will obediently censor itself. In fact, this censorship is already existing NOW, imposed by the so-called U.S. 'Liberals' and socialist do-gooders. You now 'enjoy' the same life as the Vietnamese, Cambodians, Angolans, and Nicaraguans, betrayed by you enjoy NOW. This state of social 'NORMALIZATION' may last forever, that is — your lifetime and lifetimes of you children and grandchildren . . .

IT WILL NEVER HAPPEN HERE!

What if it does happen here? Why take a chance? What are the SOLUTIONS? There are different solutions for different stages of subversion. If a nation has enough common sense to STOP subversion at the very beginning of the DEMORALIZATION stage, you may never need the painful and drastic solutions needed to deal with the CRISIS stage.

The most general solution I can offer — for the whole process of SUBVERSION — is to STOP AIDING THE SUBVERTER. You are still living in a free society and you can force your elected politicians to change their policies toward the Communist world if you so choose. But if YOU, personally do not see anything wrong in dealing with the Communists and

LOVE LETTER TO AMERICA

HELPING them in their global expansion, I feel that you should begin learning more about the reality of the Communist/ Socialist situation, not from your monopolized media, but from the independent media and press who have no vested interest in making out the Soviet Union to be the 'good guys,' and from people like myself, who have experienced Communism first-hand for many years. There are numerous American patriotic groups and organizations who are well informed and who already have many SOLUTIONS, to combat the damage done by ideological subversion some of which are as good or even better than mine. Seek these groups, join them, and DO something.

This book is my *Love Letter to America*. I did not write it to frighten or threaten the nation that I love for its freedom, its principles, its ideals. But if you were walking across the street with a friend and saw a car barreling down upon you both that your friend did not see, would you say nothing to your friend and move out of the way, leaving him to be hit? Of course, not and I do not intend to do that to you.

In my next book, I will cover the full solutions to the problem of ideological subversion. I sincerely hope you will read it.

Love,

Tomas Schuman

ABOUT THE AUTHOR

Yuri Alexandrovich Bezmenov, was a former KGB officer and journalist who worked for the Novosti Press Agency and who ultimately defected from the Soviet Union to Canada. Yuri chose freedom. Writing as Tomas Schuman in Love Letter to America, Yuri describes Soviet genocidal Communism and explains how good it is to be free.

Yuri Bezmenov aka Tomas Schuman

Made in United States
Orlando, FL
22 February 2023